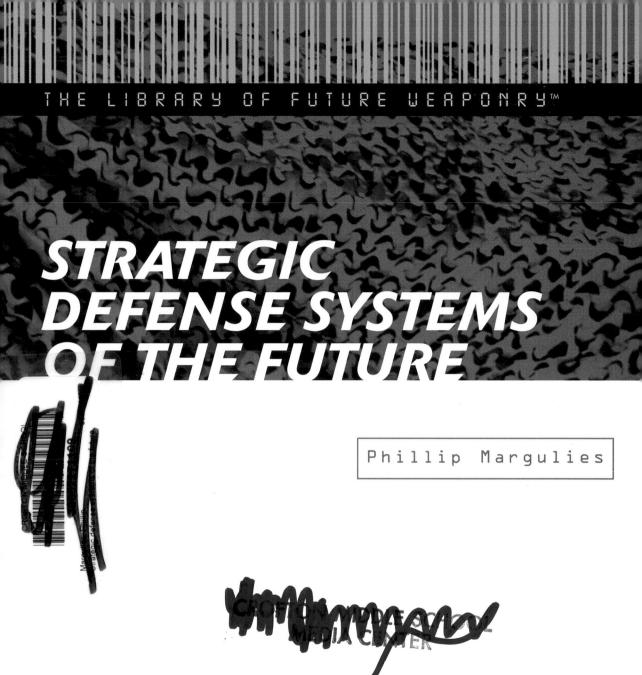

STRATEGIC DEFENSE SYSTEMS OF THE FUTURE

Phillip Margulies

The Rosen Publishing Group, Inc., New York

Published in 2006 by The Rosen Publishing Group, Inc.
29 East 21st Street, New York, NY 10010

Library of Congress Cataloging-in-Publication Data

Margulies, Phillip, 1952–
Strategic defense systems of the future / Phillip Margulies.—1st ed.
    p. cm.—(The library of future weaponry)
Includes bibliographical references and index.
ISBN 1-4042-0527-6 (library binding)
1. Ballistic missile defenses—Juvenile literature. 2. Strategic Defense
Initiative—Juvenile literature. I. Title. II. Series.

UG740.M373 2006
358.1'74—dc22

                                                                    2005017462

Manufactured in the United States of America

On the cover: A futuristic strategic defense system consisting of a satellite and missile interceptors.

CONTENTS

INTRODUCTION

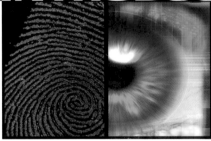

During the 1950s, American military planners began using the word "strategic" to describe the most powerful nuclear weapons. The aircraft that were always in the sky, ready for the order to drop hydrogen bombs on the Soviet Union, were called strategic bombers. They were part of the Strategic Air Command. Today, military officials and politicians speak of strategic defense systems. These are systems designed to shoot down a nuclear missile before it reaches its target. They are to be used only if the unthinkable occurs—only if a nuclear war begins.

From the moment they were first created, nuclear weapons were recognized as a grave danger to humankind. Robert Oppenheimer, head of the scientific team that built the atomic bomb, saw its first successful test in New Mexico in 1945.

Upon witnessing the power of the test bomb he quoted from Hindu scripture: "Now I am become Death, destroyer of worlds."

U.S. president Harry Truman, learning of the bomb soon after he became president, thought about the fiery destruction of Earth predicted in the Bible. Others compared the bomb to a genie that had been let out of its bottle and could never be put back. If one country could make atomic bombs, so could others. If there could be one bomb, there could be thousands. There was no returning to the world as it had been before the bomb.

In 1949, the Soviet Union successfully tested its own atomic bomb. There was little trust between the leaders of the United States and the Soviet Union, and soon the two countries were locked in a competition to make more and deadlier nuclear weapons. Each searched for faster ways to deliver the bombs to the enemy's cities. The atomic bomb was replaced by the far more powerful hydrogen bomb, and bombs were placed in missiles that could reach their targets in half an hour. For four decades, the United States and the Soviet Union faced each other like two gunslingers on a dusty street in an old Western movie. During this period, known as the Cold War, people feared that World War III might begin without warning and end life on Earth.

Nuclear war began to seem less likely in the late 1980s, when tensions eased between the United States and the Soviet Union. Both sides agreed to destroy many of their bombs and missiles. In 1991, the Soviet Union broke apart, becoming Russia and a number of other countries. With the breakup of the Soviet Union, fears of nuclear war subsided. However, both Russia and the United States still have many nuclear weapons at their disposal. In addition, six other countries have nuclear weapons: France, England, Israel, China, India, and Pakistan. North Korea claims to have nuclear weapons, but some doubt whether this is true. Other countries may have nuclear weapons in the future.

For more than sixty years, politicians, generals, and citizens have debated what to do about the nuclear threat. Is it acceptable for nations to face each other in a nuclear standoff like gangsters in a room with their guns drawn? Arms control agreements failed to prevent World War II. Can we expect them to prevent nuclear war in the future? Or can technology, which helped create this problem, provide a solution to it? That is, can we use satellites, ground radar, lasers, and high-tech rocketry to destroy nuclear weapons before they get close enough to do harm? This last option is what we mean by a strategic defense system. It's a fascinating technology, a subject of fierce debate, and a possible face of future warfare.

THE ORIGIN OF THE MISSILE THREAT

The missile threat that faced two generations of Americans grew out of a series of inventions developed during the Second World War (1939–1945). The Second World War caused the deaths of 50 million people. Most of those killed were civilians who were bombed from the air, burned in fires that incinerated whole cities, worked to death in slave labor camps, or killed in gas chambers.

The war was fought by the world's most advanced industrial powers—England, the United States, and the Soviet Union (known as the Allied forces) versus Germany, Japan, and Italy (known as the Axis powers). Every citizen had to contribute to victory, including the leading scientists who devoted their talents to weapons research. In doing so, they permanently changed the nature of war and meaning of peace.

NUCLEAR WEAPONS

In March 1939, physicist Edward Teller was at home playing Mozart on the piano when he received a phone call from Leo Szilard, a physicist in New York. "I have found the neutrons," said Szilard (as reported in *Teller's War* by William J. Broad). This meant that, according to his calculations, an incredibly powerful bomb could be made by colliding the high-energy particles found inside of uranium atoms.

Szilard also discussed his findings with another theoretical physicist, Eugene P. Wigner. Szilard, Teller, and Wigner were all Hungarian Jewish refugees who were alarmed by the rise of Adolf Hitler in Germany. They were sure that war was unavoidable. If the Germans, who were brilliant engineers, were the first to make this bomb, they might win the war. The three physicists helped persuade Albert Einstein, America's best-known scientist, to write a letter to U.S. president Franklin D. Roosevelt. In the letter, Einstein suggested that America develop the bomb first.

Under the code name Manhattan Project, the U.S. government's secret effort to build an atomic bomb continued throughout the war. By the time the first test bomb was detonated in the deserts of New Mexico on July 16, 1945, the Germans had already surrendered. The following month, two of the bombs were dropped on the Japanese cities of Hiroshima and Nagasaki, killing hundreds of thousands of Japanese civilians. The devastation caused Japan to surrender.

At 5:29 in the morning on July 16, 1945, the first atomic bomb was detonated in the New Mexico desert. Known as the Trinity Test, the blast created a mushroom-shaped cloud of smoke, fire, and debris more than seven miles (eleven kilometers) high.

Edward Teller worked on the Manhattan Project but made only minor contributions. By this time, he was distracted by another project. Realizing that the atomic bomb was inevitable, Teller became obsessed with an idea for a much more powerful weapon he called "the super." Teller's ideas would lead, in the 1950s, to the invention of the hydrogen bomb. Still later, Teller would be a dedicated advocate of strategic defense.

THE V1 AND THE V2

At the war's end it turned out that the Germans never had a program to develop an atomic bomb. But German scientists and engineers did develop secret weapons that terrorized civilian populations during the war and influenced future weaponry. Among these were the V1 and V2, short for Vergeltungswaffe 1

The V2 rocket was an early version of today's ballistic missiles produced by Germany during World War II. Over the course of the war, Germany fired more than 3,000 V2s at targets in England, Belgium, France, and the Netherlands. Above is a photograph of a V2 on display in London, England, in September 1945, about four months after Germany had surrendered.

and Vergeltungswaffe 2. In German, *Vergeltungswaffe* means "vengeance weapon."

The V1 was a flying bomb that used a jet engine for propulsion and a mechanical autopilot for guidance. In 1944, thousands of V1 missiles were aimed at London. The V1 missiles traveled at low altitudes and made a distinctive sound that led people to call them buzz bombs. Their approach could be seen for miles, but they were so fast that antiaircraft guns could seldom hit them. Eventually, though, engineers found a way to counter the V1. They equipped artillery shells with sensing devices that made the shells explode when they were close to the V1.

RADAR ENTERS THE PICTURE

The sensing devices used radar (short for "radio detecting and ranging"), another technology developed in the Second World War. Radar can locate enemy vehicles and weapons by bouncing radio waves off the surfaces of hard objects. Radar gave the United States and England a crucial advantage against German aircraft during the war. The radar- artillery shells used against the V1 are the ancestors of today's missiles defenses.

No countermeasure was found during the war for the V2, Germany's other missile system. The V2 was a rocket. It traveled straight up, nearly reaching outside the atmosphere. It came down at speeds greater than the speed of sound.

MISSILES PLUS NUCLEAR WEAPONS

After the Allies marched into Germany in 1945, German scientists were brought back to the United States and the Soviet Union to work for the victors, developing rockets and missiles. For people who thought about the weapons of the future, it was obvious that nuclear weapons and missiles like the V1 or V2 would make a terrifying combination. The army's War Department Equipment Board (referred to as the Stilwell Board because it was chaired by General Joseph Stilwell) evaluated the future uses of these new weapons. On May 29, 1946, the secret Stilwell Board Report advised the

U.S. government to prepare a defense against nuclear-tipped missiles. The report stated:

> Guided missiles traveling at extreme altitudes and at velocities in excess of supersonic speed are inevitable. Intercontinental ranges of more than 3,000 miles [4,828 kilometers] and payloads sufficient to carry atomic explosives are to be expected. Remotely controlled, and equipped with homing devices designed to be attracted to sound, metal, or heat, such missiles would be incapable of interception with any existing equipment such as fighter aircraft and antiaircraft fire. Guided interceptor missiles, dispatched in accordance with electronically computed data obtained from radar detection stations, will be required.

By the 1960s, one prediction of the Stilwell report had come

A Minuteman III nuclear missile rests in a silo near Cheyenne, Wyoming. As of 2005, the United States had 500 Minuteman III missiles in its inventory, each capable of hitting targets as far away as 8,000 miles (13,000 km). The Minuteman is a type of missile known as an ICBM, or intercontinental ballistic missile.

FISSION AND FUSION

The atomic bomb and the hydrogen bomb harness the energy that holds atoms together. At the center of the atom is the nucleus, consisting of tiny particles called protons and neutrons. Some unstable elements called radioactive isotopes contain extra neutrons. Over time, they release these extra neutrons, along with energy.

In 1939, two German scientists, Otto Hahn and Fritz Strassman, used the neutrons emitted by radioactive isotopes to split uranium atoms. This reaction was called fission.

The fission of the uranium atom caused the release of additional neutrons, which could be used to split other uranium atoms in a chain reaction. Leo Szilard and Edward Teller realized that if large amounts of radioactive material were put together, this chain reaction could result in the release of enormous amounts of energy. Their idea became the basis for the atomic bomb.

While working to create the atomic bomb, physicists speculated about another type of nuclear reaction. In this reaction, the atoms would be joined together, or fused. This would result in an even greater release of energy than splitting the atoms. Enrico Fermi, winner of the 1938 Nobel Peace Prize in Physics, wondered if the heat from an exploding atomic bomb might be used to trigger a fusion reaction. Fermi's idea launched his colleague Edward Teller on the intellectual obsession that would lead to the creation of the first hydrogen bomb in 1952.

true—nuclear missiles had been created. However, missile defense systems had been designed and tested, but so far none of them worked.

Meanwhile, in hidden silos across the Soviet Union and the United States, and in the oceans on nuclear submarines, thousands of guided missiles were ready to be launched at the enemy. These missiles were armed with hydrogen bombs, each 1,000 to 10,000 times more powerful than the bombs that destroyed Hiroshima and Nagasaki. Once they were launched, nothing could stop them.

MUTUALLY ASSURED DESTRUCTION

Neither the United States nor the Soviet Union had any defense against these ballistic missiles. However, they did have something that could prevent an attack. They had the guarantee of a return attack. Once an attack was detected, the nation being attacked could launch enough nuclear weapons to destroy the attacker. The Soviet Union could obliterate the United States in a matter of hours if it wished, but the Soviet Union would be obliterated, too. Even if it struck first, it couldn't prevent the United States from launching warheads in retaliation. For both nations, starting a nuclear war would be suicide.

American defense secretary Robert MacNamara gave a name to this situation. He called it Mutually Assured Destruction. To many, it seemed appropriate that the initial letters of this phrase spelled out the word MAD. Surely, there was something insane about it.

THE STRATEGIC DEFENSE INITIATIVE

Although the United States did not have a defense against ballistic missiles by the late 1960s, it wasn't for lack of trying. In 1946, the United States hired private companies to test V2 rockets in search of ways to intercept them. The likeliest weapon to use against a missile going faster than the speed of sound would be another missile. These missiles, known as antiballistic missiles, would either have to explode close to the enemy missile or actually strike it in midflight. Radar would guide it to its target. It would be like hitting a bullet with a bullet.

Both the Soviet Union and the United States worked on antiballistic missile systems constantly throughout the 1950s and 1960s. In the United States, the programs changed names many times as the science and the strategy behind them changed: Projects Thumper and Wizard (1946); the

Nike-Zeus Project (1957); the Sentinel Antiballistic System (1967), which would have used nuclear explosions to destroy incoming ballistic missiles; and Safeguard (1975), which was the only system to become operational.

ANTIMISSILES CAN'T GET OFF THE GROUND

All of these projects were experimental. None of them ever produced antimissile systems good enough to make a difference in the outcome of a nuclear war. By the early 1970s, most experts had decided that missile defense would probably not work, and even if it did it would be a bad idea. Missile defense might make one side or both think that if it struck first it could use its defensive missiles to foil the enemy's counterattack and win the war. Plus, a missile defense system would be very expensive.

In 1972, U.S. president Richard Nixon and Soviet general secretary Leonid Brezhnev signed the Antiballistic Missile (ABM) Treaty. This agreement limited the United States and the Soviet Union to a small number of antiballistic missiles and limited the research that could be done on missile defense.

EDWARD TELLER AND THE REVIVAL OF MISSILE DEFENSE

The scientist Edward Teller, often called the father of the hydrogen bomb, spent most of his life working on nuclear weapons. He was convinced that missile defense could work. He also believed that despite the ABM Treaty, the Soviet Union was developing a missile defense system. For Teller, treaties

On May 26, 1972, the United States and the Soviet Union agreed to the Antiballistic Missile (ABM) Treaty. In the photograph above, U.S. President Richard Nixon *(left)* shakes hands with the Soviet Union's Leonid Brezhnev after signing the document. In June 2002, the United States withdrew from the ABM Treaty. Since then, the United States government has increased its effort to build a strategic defense system.

with the Soviets were worthless. Only better technology could make the United States secure and give U.S. leaders the confidence to counter the Soviet threat.

In 1967, future U.S. president Ronald Reagan visited the top-secret Lawrence Livermore National Laboratory in California. At the time, Reagan was the governor of California. At Livermore, Teller led teams of American scientists in the development of nuclear weapons and in the research of laser fusion (using lasers and fusion reactions to generate energy). Reagan shared Teller's faith in technology as well as his distrust of treaties with the Soviet Union. Conversations with Teller helped convince

The Lawrence Livermore National Laboratory has been involved in missile defense research for decades. Pictured above is the target chamber of the laboratory's National Ignition Facility (NIF). The NIF creates high-energy lasers that allow scientists to perform experiments at extreme temperatures and pressures. Although it is not a stated goal of the NIF, research done there could be valuable in designing future X-ray lasers for missile defense.

Reagan that with continued research, an effective missile defense system could be built.

THE BIRTH OF THE X-RAY LASER

Reagan was already planning to scrap the ABM Treaty and return to strategic defense when he ran for president in 1980. In November of that year, immediately after the election, scientists from the Lawrence Livermore laboratory conducted a secret experiment beneath the Nevada desert. This experiment

In the 1980s, the Nova X-ray laser facility at the Lawrence Livermore Laboratory produced the world's most powerful laser beam. Nova, which cost 176 million dollars to build, took up four separate rooms, the largest of which was almost the length of a football field. Nova was shut down in 1999, but many of its parts have since then been incorporated into new laser research facilities.

would change the shape of Reagan's strategic defense proposal. The experiment proved that a nuclear explosion using a hydrogen bomb could be used to power an X-ray laser that was far more powerful than any laser in existence.

In Teller's view, the X-ray laser would make it possible to destroy enemy nuclear weapons within seconds after they were launched. A nuclear explosion in space would power multiple X-ray lasers, which would target and destroy the enemy missiles. Instead of trying to hit a bullet with a bullet, this system would detect the enemy weapons at launch from outer space. The system would strike with perfect accuracy by means of high-energy rays that traveled at the speed of light.

REAGAN'S PROPOSAL

In a televised speech on March 23, 1983, President Reagan proposed a new antimissile policy. "What if free people could live secure in the knowledge that their security did not rest upon the threat of instant U.S. retaliation to deter a Soviet attack, that we could intercept and destroy strategic ballistic missiles before they reached our soil or that of our allies? Would it not be better to save lives than to avenge them?"

Reagan called his proposal the Strategic Defense Initiative (SDI), "a defensive shield that won't hurt people but will knock down nuclear weapons before they can hurt people . . . Some say it will bring war to the heavens. But its purpose is to deter war in the heavens and on earth."

THE DEBATE OVER STRATEGIC DEFENSE

The SDI was controversial, mainly because it interfered with existing nuclear arms treaties. Critics of the SDI argued that it would make nuclear war more likely. They were especially troubled by the idea of orbiting X-ray lasers powered by hydrogen bombs. Would there now be nuclear weapons in outer space? If the Soviet Union and the United States started competing with each other to put defensive nuclear devices in orbit, what would prevent them from putting offensive nuclear weapons in orbit? Also, the SDI was an incredibly expensive project. Some critics worried that it might negatively affect the nation's economy.

SDI's defenders argued that missile defense was essential for the nation's security. They believed that when nations had the ability to destroy each other, it was only a matter of time before a technical mistake, or the act of a madman, or an international crisis would lead to nuclear war. Teller suggested that an X-ray laser would not have to be deployed in space—it could "pop up," that is, be launched from a submarine when an attack began, and then target the enemy missiles.

HOW MANY BOMBS?

A modern nuclear weapon is 1,000 to 10,000 times more powerful than the bomb that destroyed the Japanese city of Hiroshima. In 1985, before the United States and the Soviet Union agreed to reduce the number of their weapons, each country had about 10,000 weapons aimed at the other. The United States had about 2,000 nuclear warheads on land-based intercontinental ballistic missiles (ICBM), 5,000 on submarine-launched missiles, and 3,000 on air-to-surface missiles and air-launched cruise missiles. The Soviet Union had about 6,500 nuclear warheads on land-based ICBMs, 2,000 on submarine-launched missiles, and 1,000 on air-to-surface missiles and air-launched cruise missiles.

The quest for effective missile defense continues in the United States today. Above is a photograph from inside the Joint National Integration Center, part of the Missile Defense Agency, where military specialists test components of a future ballistic missile defense system.

As it turned out, X-ray lasers had military flaws that prevented them from playing a key role in future missile defense. The pop-up idea caused delays that made it difficult for the X-ray lasers to hit missiles early. In addition, X-ray lasers would have difficulty penetrating the atmosphere. Though billions of dollars were spent on X-ray laser development, military planners soon began viewing other devices as better options for strategic defense.

THE FALL OF THE SOVIET UNION

Some people believe that the SDI helped bring about the fall of the Soviet Union. The cost of the Soviet Union's existing weapon systems was already stretching the country's weak economy to the limit. The Soviets could not afford the added expense of an elaborate new missile defense system. Under the leadership of Mikhail Gorbachev, who came to power in 1985, the Soviet Union gradually became a more open society. In the late 1980s, for the first time since the beginning of the Cold War, the United States and the Soviet Union agreed to sharply reduce the size of their nuclear stockpiles.

In 1991, the Soviet Union broke apart because its leaders were no longer willing to hold it together by force. The Soviet Union's remaining nuclear bombs and missiles were inherited by the Russian Federation.

THE BASICS
OF A STRATEGIC
DEFENSE SYSTEM

Critics of strategic defense systems often say that it will turn outer space into a battlefield. Defenders point out that space is already a battlefield. Take artificial satellites: there are now thousands of satellites in orbit over Earth. They are essential to modern telecommunication, and their destruction would have a serious impact on a nation's economy. Other satellites are the military's eyes in the sky. Ground and air forces rely on them to see the battlefield from space. These satellites would be targets in a war with any technologically advanced opponent.

Even before satellites became so important for communications and warfare, space became a battlefield with the invention of modern ballistic missiles. These rockets achieve their speed by rising to altitudes above the atmosphere, where air pressure no longer acts as a drag on the flight of the missile.

THE PRIMARY TARGET: THE BALLISTIC MISSILE

A typical ballistic missile is between 30 and 100 feet tall (9.1 to 30.5 meters). It can accelerate up to 15,000 miles (24,140 km) per hour. Missiles are built to be light to help them reach these high speeds while carrying several thousand pounds of payload.

In the future, missiles might become heavier to counter missile defense. They could be given stronger armor to protect them from antiballistic missiles. This process is called hardening. Giving them this extra armor makes the missiles slower. However, engineers in the future may come up with new ways to harden missiles without sacrificing speed.

Most ballistic missiles bear a strong resemblance to the multi-stage rockets that carry astronauts and satellites into orbit. Like

A Minuteman III leaves an impressive trail of thick smoke during blastoff. The missile uses three separate engines to provide it with enough power to climb to a height of 700 miles (1,120 km). During its flight, the Minuteman III reaches a top speed of about 15,000 miles (24,140 km) per hour.

these space rockets, they discard their earlier stages when no longer needed. From launch to target, their flight is divided into four phases.

PHASES OF A BALLISTIC MISSILE

During the first, or boost, phase the missile's engines burn for up to 300 seconds until the missile is about 200 miles (322 km) above Earth. The first 50 seconds of this flight takes the missile to where the atmosphere is too thin to be a drag on the missile. It quickly accelerates to its top speed. At the end of the boost phase, the engine drops off to decrease the weight of the missile.

The postboost phase follows the boost phase. How the missile behaves now depends on whether it contains one warhead or many. A single-warhead missile simply directs itself to its target. Many missiles contain multiple warheads; some have as many as ten. As the postboost phase begins, multiple-warhead missiles begin to release them one by one. Each warhead is directed at a different target. It may also spread decoys, made of balloons or tinfoil, and chaff, made of small pieces of wire or aluminum. These are designed to defeat an antimissile system. The postboost phase may last until the missile reaches the top of the trajectory some 700 miles (1,120 km) above Earth.

Following postboost is the midcourse phase. This phase of a ballistic missile's flight lasts around twenty minutes. During this period, the decoys that were released earlier travel alongside heavy warheads, undisturbed by air. Radar systems find it difficult to distinguish between a decoy and a warhead because their surfaces reflect radio waves similarly.

The last five minutes of the flight make up the terminal phase. There isn't much time now to destroy the missile, but this last phase offers some advantages to the defenders. The chaff would be gone because the thin metallic foil strips would not be heavy enough to fall as fast as the warheads. The decoys would also tend to fall and move differently, enabling radar and satellite systems to identify the warheads. At a preset altitude, when the warhead's own radar tells it that it is close enough to its target, the warhead will explode. It may also explode when its sensors indicate that it is going to be hit by an antimissile. If the warhead explodes when it is 20 miles (32 km) or more above Earth, there may be no immediate damage to life or property.

A SHIELD AGAINST MISSILES

In his initial speech about the Strategic Defense Initiative, Ronald Reagan compared it to a shield. The comparison is correct in that the goal of missile defense is to stop or deflect an attack, much as a shield stops the thrust of a sword. The word "shield" is misleading, however, for anyone who thinks of missile defense as an impenetrable dome over the country. In reality, missile defenses would involve many parts, acting separately and together, to counteract attacks coming from many directions.

The most complete and elaborate missile defense, like the one President Reagan had in mind in the 1980s, would be able

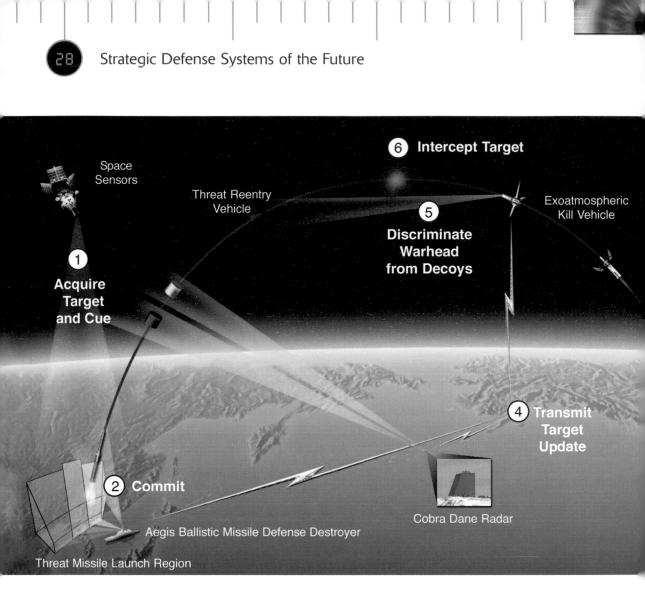

6 Intercept Target

Space Sensors

Threat Reentry Vehicle

Exoatmospheric Kill Vehicle

5 Discriminate Warhead from Decoys

1 Acquire Target and Cue

4 Transmit Target Update

2 Commit

Cobra Dane Radar

Aegis Ballistic Missile Defense Destroyer

Threat Missile Launch Region

to defend against a massive nuclear attack by an enemy like the former Soviet Union. It would also be able to defend a small missile attack by a less technologically advanced nation or terrorist group.

SERIES OF LAYERED DEFENSES

Thinking in terms of the worst, most difficult case—an all-out, massive attack—designers of strategic defense systems plan to

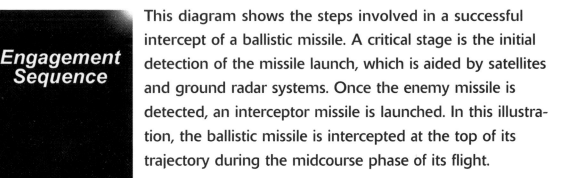

Engagement Sequence

This diagram shows the steps involved in a successful intercept of a ballistic missile. A critical stage is the initial detection of the missile launch, which is aided by satellites and ground radar systems. Once the enemy missile is detected, an interceptor missile is launched. In this illustration, the ballistic missile is intercepted at the top of its trajectory during the midcourse phase of its flight.

Joint National Integration Center

Launch Interceptor

protect the United States with a series of layered defenses. Each layer will target a different phase in the flight of the enemy's missiles.

In the first layer, systems such as spy satellites, ground radar, or infrared detectors (sensors that work by detecting heat) detect ballistic missiles at the moment of launch, during the boost phase. The boost phase is considered the best time for destroying ballistic missiles for several reasons. At this point, the ballistic missile's bulky engines are still attached, presenting a larger, more vulnerable target. The walls of the engines are lighter and easier to penetrate than the walls of the warheads. The missiles at launch also produce intense heat and light, making detection easier. Defensive weapons in the form of ground, air, or space-based antimissile missiles (which explode when they get close to the target), lasers, or kinetic energy weapons (weapons that collide with the ballistic missile) immediately destroy them.

NORAD—WATCHING THE SKIES

The North American Aerospace Defense Command (NORAD) was established in 1958. Using data from satellites and ground-based radar, NORAD monitors and warns of attack by aircraft, missiles, or space vehicles. NORAD also provides surveillance and control of the airspace of Canada and the United States.

NORAD maintains operations bases in Colorado; Washington; New York; Florida; Alaska; and Ontario, Canada. Its best-known location is a fortified military facility in a hollowed-out mountain in Colorado. According to William J. Broad in his book *Teller's War*, the top-secret facility resembles the villain's lair in a James Bond movie.

A visitor walks past a three-feet-thick, heavily fortified door inside the Cheyenne Mountain Operations Center in Colorado. NORAD shares the facility with USNORTHCOM, an organization created after the September 11 terrorist attacks to assist with homeland defense.

"There's a big steel door into the mountain and a huge subterranean complex carved inside. In the war room there's a map of the United States that can show the paths of incoming planes and missiles."

At the height of the Cold War, NORAD's mission was to detect an enemy nuclear attack. In the age of missile defense, NORAD expects to help locate and target the enemy missiles that defenses intend to destroy.

Early in the boost phase, a missile is full of rocket fuel. If hit it would probably explode. Hit early enough, it would fall back to the place where it was launched. Hit late in the boost phase, its pieces would continue to travel across great distances but would miss their targets. Also, the warheads would likely not be armed since arming typically occurs after the postboost phase. Even if they landed on their targets, they would be duds.

In the postboost phase, missiles are much harder to detect because they do not emit enough energy to be seen by the sensors in spy satellites. Instead, the sensors will calculate their positions from observations made during the boost phase. Based on this information, lasers and kinetic energy weapons would be used to target the postboost-phase missile.

In the midcourse phase, strategic defense would rely on an exoatmospheric kill vehicle (EKV), a package of sensors, computers and rocket thrusters around 5 feet (1.5 m) in length. The EKV would be launched on top of an interceptor rocket, then home in on the warhead and destroy it by colliding with it.

An Arrow 2 interceptor blasts off from a mobile launcher in a test on July 29, 2004, at Point Mugu Sea Range in California. The Arrow 2 is part of a joint missile defense program between the United States and Israel. This test resulted in a successful intercept of its target. More tests are planned for the future.

The terminal phase is the last layer of defense. The interceptors used during this phase have to be able to operate within the atmosphere. Their rapid travel through the atmosphere will generate intense heat, making guidance difficult. Some interceptors designed for this phase collide with the vehicle, while others would release a small nuclear device when close to the target warhead.

INTERCEPTORS

At every stage of the layered defense, a combination of different defensive weapons would be used to stop the missiles. While some weapons systems are designed with a specific phase of the ballistic missile's flight in mind, most weapons are expected to work in more than one layer of defense. The various antimissiles, known as interceptors, can be roughly classed by their location in space or on Earth.

Space-based interceptors would be placed in permanent orbit over Earth. Space-based interceptors might consist of kinetic energy weapons, lasers, or particle beams (weapons that use electric fields to propel neutrons or other subatomic particles to near light speeds). Space-based interceptors have a liability: they are highly visible to the enemy and vulnerable to attack.

Ground-based interceptors are lasers, particle beams, and missiles located on the ground, on submarines, or on aircraft. Some ground-based interceptors are kinetic energy weapons, which must make direct contact with their targets. Others would explode when they are near enough to enemy missiles to destroy them. Some would use nuclear explosions to destroy enemy missiles while they are still outside the atmosphere.

A peculiar property of lasers creates a third category: ground/ space with mirrors. Lasers can be deflected and redirected with mirrors. It would be easier to place a large, heavy, powerful laser on Earth and direct it to its target through a series of mirror relays located in space.

TOOLS OF STRATEGIC DEFENSE

Scientists, politicians, and military leaders continue to debate whether strategic defense systems will be effective, and whether a race to produce them is a good idea. One thing no one disputes, though, is their beauty as gadgets. The challenge of defeating a rocket equipped with a guidance system and traveling at 15,000 miles (24,140 km) per hour has brought out a great deal of creativity in America's scientists and engineers.

DETECTING A NUCLEAR ATTACK

Time is everything in missile defense. A sneak attack is the most likely kind of attack at the beginning of a nuclear war. This element of surprise is necessary to knock out the opponent's ability to retaliate with nuclear weapons of its own.

The Midcourse Space Experiment (MSX) satellite has been orbiting Earth since 1996. It was designed to detect ballistic missiles during the midcourse phase of flight. Pictured at left is the MSX satellite shortly before it was launched from Vandenberg Air Force Base in California.

Because of this, the military has made it a priority to get the earliest possible warning of a nuclear weapon launch.

The development of orbital satellites in the 1950s and 1960s made this task easier. Satellites are objects outside the atmosphere (sometimes just outside the atmosphere, and sometimes at distances greater than the diameter of Earth). They travel fast enough so that there is a balance between Earth's gravitational field and the forces propelling them forward. If the satellites were to slow down significantly, they would fall. If they were to speed up enough, they would fly out into space.

Since Earth rotates very fast, it's possible for a satellite to be traveling fast enough to stay in orbit and yet stay in the same spot over Earth. This is called geostationary orbit. Satellites in

The U.S. military hopes to launch two satellites in early 2007 as part of an experimental missile defense system. The satellites are designed to detect ballistic missiles, track them, and then pass that information on to missile defense interceptors. The above illustration shows what the two satellites will look like from their perch high above Earth.

geostationary orbit must be located very far from Earth for this effect to occur.

EARLY WARNING SATELLITES AND GLOBAL POSITIONING SYSTEM

Satellites are a vital part of the early warning system for strategic defense. From space, around 22,000 miles (35,406 km) above Earth, geostationary satellites are positioned over the countries from which a nuclear attack is most likely. They are aided by the United States' Ballistic Missile Early Warning System, a radar network on the ground. Working together, the satellite and the ground-based radar systems could not only detect the launch the moment it occurred but also figure out the targets.

Satellites must be able to distinguish between a nuclear launch, the launch of a rocket carrying a satellite, and the launch of a missile that is merely being tested and is not aimed at a target. The U.S. military also uses global-positioning-system satellites to track movements of all kinds on Earth, with special attention to the movements of all weapons. Military commanders already use these satellites to pinpoint targets.

Better warning and tracking systems are in development. The next generation of early warning satellites is called Space-Based Infrared System High. As the name implies, this system detects infrared rays, the low-frequency radiation given off by heated objects. Computers help sort the information into a meaningful picture of events on Earth. Ultimately, a tracking system like this would not only provide early warning of missile launches but also provide interceptors with information to locate and destroy them.

KINETIC ENERGY INTERCEPTORS

"Kinetic energy interceptors" (KEIs) is the most recent name for the oldest approach to destroying missiles. Using KEIs is the equivalent of hitting a bullet with a bullet, or destroying a missile by direct contact with another missile. They're more

A kinetic energy interceptor is prepared for a test launch in December 2001. The goal of the test was to intercept a dummy intercontinental ballistic missile that had been launched from an air force base in California. The inset shows the interceptor's kill vehicle, a device that releases from the interceptor after launch and seeks out the enemy ballistic missile. The U.S. military will continue to perform similar tests in the future in order to perfect the interceptor technology.

sophisticated than ever, but they also have a harder job than ever—the closing speed of a ballistic missile may be as much as 22,000 miles (35,406 km) per hour.

KEIs were initially seen as last-ditch weapons that would attempt to hit missiles already descending toward their target on Earth. Today military planners envision launching KEIs from submarines and aircraft near enemy territory to intercept missiles in the boost phase as well as during the midcourse phase.

Kinetic energy interceptors rise into the air from launchers and are propelled by booster rockets in three stages. These booster rockets are similar to those of the spacecraft that hurled the Apollo astronauts to the moon, and to the rockets that launch long-range missiles.

The KEIs currently being developed in the United States will be 36 feet, 4 inches long (11.1 m), and 36 inches (91 centimeters) in diameter. They will reach a speed of nearly 4 miles (6.4 km) per second in less than 60 seconds. After the three stages of the rocket have dropped off, future KEIs will release multiple "kill vehicles" (just as the ballistic missiles themselves release multiple reentry vehicles, each bearing a warhead). The kill vehicles will be equipped with computerized guidance systems and rockets that will enable them to home in on their fast-moving targets.

LASERS IN MISSILE DEFENSE

The word "laser" is an acronym for "light amplification by stimulated emission of radiation." Light is ordinarily emitted

MISSILE DEFENSE AGENCY AND ITS CONTRACTORS

The Missile Defense Agency (MDA) is the arm of the United States Defense Department responsible for developing, testing, and preparing the United States' missile defense system. The MDA's motto is "Making Ballistic Missile Defense a Reality."

In 2005, the MDA had a budget of between 7 and 8 billion dollars. While the Missile Defense Agency oversees the development of weapons systems and helps set the goals, the actual work of weapons development is done by private companies. The MDA contracts much of the work on strategic missile defense to aerospace companies like Boeing, Lockheed Martin, and Northrop Grumman. These large government contracts benefit the companies and benefit the economy of the states in which the companies are located.

in a group of waves and particles in many different frequencies and in many different directions. Lasers are devices that produce "coherent light," or light of one frequency aimed in one direction.

The first functioning laser was demonstrated in 1960. Since then, lasers have proved themselves useful in many areas, from surgery to printing to the reading of CD-ROMs in home computers. Though the *l* in "laser" stands for "light," lasers can work with other frequencies of electromagnetic radiation, including microwaves. The higher the frequency of radiation a laser uses, the more energy its beam can carry.

Since laser beams travel in a sharp, defined line for great distances and can transmit enormous amounts of energy, their potential as an antimissile weapon has long been recognized. Whether they turn out to be effective for strategic defense, battle-field lasers are certainly coming.

TRANSFORMING THE BATTLEFIELD WITH LASERS

Strategic defense lasers in development today are mounted on jumbo jets. They will receive information from satellites, ground radar, and the jet's own systems to direct themselves at enemy missiles. The lasers will rupture the missiles' casing and cause them to lose power or flight control. In the more distant future, lasers may be mounted on satellite battle stations, where they would be able to shoot down enemy missiles in the boost phase.

Right now, lasers powerful enough to be used as weapons are extremely heavy. They probably will become light enough one day to be used on vehicles less cumbersome than a jumbo jet. If lasers do turn out to work as weapons, they will be used for many war-fighting purposes besides zapping ballistic missiles. They have the potential to transform the battlefield of the future. Fighter jets and gunships may use lasers, allowing them to hit

This is an artist's conception of the Airborne Laser, which is a Boeing 747-400F commercial airliner modified to carry a high-energy laser. The weapon is designed to intercept ballistic missiles in the boost phase. It is currently in the testing stage. The military hopes to have a working version in the air by 2008.

targets with incredible precision and controlled force. Even ballistic missiles themselves may be armed with lasers to defend themselves as they move toward their targets.

PARTICLE BEAMS

Particle beams are streams of atoms or subatomic particles accelerated to nearly the speed of light. For nearly half a century, nuclear physicists have been speeding up particles by means of powerful magnets in particle accelerators. Streams of particles accelerated to speeds near that of light would make a very powerful weapon.

So far, existing particle accelerators are enormous. Some scientists maintain that a machine pushing particles to speeds approaching that of light would need to be 2 miles (3.2 km) long and 4 miles (6.4 km) wide. A machine capable of accelerating particles to half the speed of light would weigh 500 tons (454 metric tons). Right now it's hard to imagine these machines being lifted into space, so they remain an option only for the distant future.

HOW A STRATEGIC DEFENSE SYSTEM MIGHT FAIL

Opponents of strategic defense systems see arms control treaties, not technology, as the best way of assuring the United States' security. They point out that a shield that permits one side to shoot weapons at the other without concern for retaliation could lead to a renewed arms race, and perhaps trigger an unnecessary war.

In addition, opponents say that those who favor strategic defense are far too optimistic about its potential for assuring the survival of a nation after a nuclear attack.

HOLES IN THE SYSTEM?

Some critics of the original SDI plan called it a Maginot Line in space. The Maginot Line was a system of fortified positions the French built after World War I (1914–1918) to protect against an attack by their aggressive neighbor,

Germany. When the Second World War came, the Germans simply circled around the Maginot Line. They reached Paris, and forced France to surrender, something they had not been able to accomplish in the earlier war. The moral of this story is that military defenses don't prevent war, they simply change the enemy's war plan.

It has been more than twenty years since U.S. president Ronald Reagan first proposed the SDI, and an effective strategic missile defense system is still a work in progress. None of its components have managed to do their job in anything like battle conditions. Critics call the tests that have been done so far "strapped chicken" tests, or unrealistic tests on easy targets. In eight tests conducted between 1999 and 2004, antiballistic missiles hit five of their targets, and missed three. In two more recent tests, they failed to launch at all, making the success rate 50 percent.

An antiballistic missile separates from its booster during a flight test in August 2000. A failure in booster separation is one example of the many things that can go wrong between the ignition of the missile's engine and destruction of the incoming ballistic missile.

There is no doubt that with enough money the technology of missile defense will improve. Unfortunately, so will the technology of the missiles the defense system is designed to intercept.

NOT 100 PERCENT EFFECTIVE

The most unrealistic aspect of Ronald Reagan's SDI was the suggestion that it would make the people of the United States safe from nuclear attack. To do this, the system would have to be foolproof. It would have to work 100 percent of the time. If it worked 99 percent of the time during an all-out war between two nuclear superpowers, then several hydrogen bombs could reach us. The ensuing explosions and radioactive fallout would kill several million people and make some of our most populous states uninhabitable for many years.

What prevents a missile defense from being 100 percent effective? Nothing is ever 100 percent effective, especially in war, a high-stakes competition between opponents trying to outwit each other. As anyone who has played chess or checkers or any other competitive game knows, the opponent doesn't just sit there while you make several moves in a row. The enemy is clever, too, and responds to what you do. Missile defenses will face specific countermeasures that are designed to make them fail at least some of the time.

DECOYS AND CHAFF THAT PRETEND TO BE WARHEADS

Any antimissile device, whether it's a kinetic energy interceptor, a laser, or a particle beam, has a job that's incredibly difficult. It has to hit and disable an object going at supersonic speeds. To make the job even harder the enemy will present extra objects to intercept, such as chaff that confuses sensors and decoys that look like warheads. In addition, some warheads will be made to resemble decoys by, for example, enclosing them in metal-coated balloons. How will missile defenses respond to the possibility that the warheads may resemble decoys, while the decoys may resemble warheads? They may simply have to hit everything in sight. This will make their job harder, and very expensive. It is much cheaper to build a decoy than to build an interceptor.

It is true that with time and money the technology for detecting warheads among chaff and decoys will improve. However, so will the technology for evading the missile defenses, including better decoys and better disguises for the warheads. The ballistic missile is a moving target in more than one sense: as missile defenses improve, so will the ballistic missiles.

THE VULNERABILITY OF SPACE-BASED DEFENSES

The original centerpiece of Reagan's SDI proposal, a space-based X-ray laser, was gradually sidelined from plans for strategic defense. The reason for this was not that the X-ray laser was technologically impossible, though it does remain decades away from practical use even today. The X-ray laser was sidelined because planners in the Reagan administration gradually realized that an orbiting defense system would be

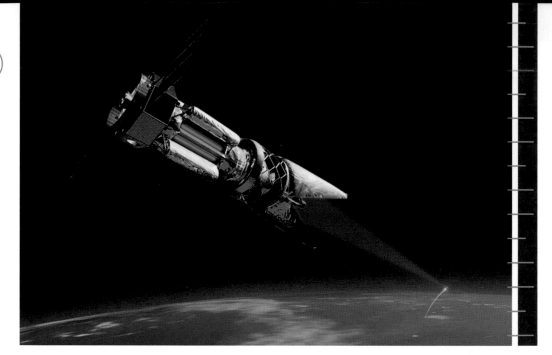

The goal of a space-based laser is to strike an enemy's missile early in its ascent. The U.S. Air Force hoped to have an experimental version of a space-based laser ready by 2012, but that date has been pushed back indefinitely. Above is an artist's rendering of what a space-based laser might look like in the future.

extremely vulnerable to attack at the outset of a nuclear war. It would be the first target of the opponent's X-ray laser, because the opponent would eventually have one too.

In fact, the X-ray laser, if it worked, would function better as an attack weapon against objects in space than as a defender knocking out missiles being launched on Earth. The atmosphere of Earth tends to distort and weaken lasers. In the vacuum of space, lasers are at their best. A working X-ray laser would be ideal for destroying an opponent's early warning and tracking satellites, space-based battle stations, and X-ray lasers.

One day, space-based weapons like the X-ray laser might also prove useful for attacking the known location of ground missile

THE PATRIOT MISSILE IN THE GULF WAR

During the Gulf War, the United States' first war in Iraq in 1991, the antiballistic Patriot missile briefly came into play. It was used against the Scud missiles that Saddam Hussein was launching into Israel and Saudi Arabia.

In a visit to the Raytheon factory, in Andover, Massachusetts, where the Patriot missiles were made, President George H. W. Bush praised the record of the Patriot in Israel. It was "41 for 42; 42 Scuds engaged, 41 intercepted." This statistic was often repeated. However, according to Israeli investigators, this statement is false. Richard Dean Burns and Lester H. Brune reported in their book *The Quest for Missile Defenses* that a team of Israeli investigators found that there was "no clear evidence of even a single successful intercept" of a Scud by a Patriot.

These conflicting claims prove that in warfare it's often very difficult to determine the effectiveness of a weapon. Often, statistics about casualties and reports of damage done to a target will vary widely, depending on who is doing the reporting.

defenses, including ground radar. They would give the opponents in a nuclear arms race what military planners call a first strike capability. They would add to the military advantage of striking first in a nuclear war, therefore, making nuclear war more likely.

The SBX-1 radar is seen under construction in this photograph taken in June 2005. The Missile Defense Agency has spent 815 million dollars to build the radar, which will be a vital feature of tomorrow's national missile defense system. The radar is being constructed in Texas. When finished, it will be mounted on an oil rig off the coast of Alaska.

Weapons in space will never provide a foolproof defensive shield. They should be thought of as additional guns that the nations of the world will be able to point at each other in the nuclear standoff that has existed since the early 1950s. From that time until the present day, many believe that the biggest step the United States made toward safety was the arms reduction agreements made between the United States and the Soviet Union during the 1980s and 1990s. In the future, further arms control agreements, and not missile defense, may be the best way to ensure the country's safety.

THE CHANGING DEBATE

Since the mid-1980s, politics and scientific developments have changed the debate on strategic defense for both its advocates and its opponents. The Soviet Union has disappeared, and its nuclear weapons are in the hands of the Russian Federation. China, India, Pakistan, and perhaps North Korea have developed nuclear weapons of their own. It is feared that Iran may join them soon. The immediate threat to the United States has changed in ways that make strategic defense seem in some ways more practical, in some ways less.

On the one hand, strategic defense would probably have much more success in defending against an attack from an aggressive yet technologically inferior opponent like North Korea than it would have in defending against an attack by another nuclear superpower. Because of its limited resources, North Korea would not be able to launch a massive strike that would overwhelm a strategic defense shield. And after all, it's not impossible that someone like Kim Jong Il, North Korea's unpredictable leader, might one day do something as crazy as launch a missile strike against the United States. In that event, a missile defense might prevent a tragedy, enabling the United States to protect itself without inflicting a nuclear counterstrike on North Korea's downtrodden citizens.

THE THREAT OF TERRORISM

On the other hand, terrorism seems to be the most immediate threat to the security of the United States today. Americans

U.S. secretary of state Madeleine Albright faces North Korean ruler Kim Jong Il in this photograph taken on October 23, 2000. For many years, U.S. leaders have had a tense relationship with Kim Jong Il. His claim that North Korea has nuclear weapons has underscored the importance of future peace talks between these two countries.

worry about what would happen if nuclear weapons fell into the hands of terrorists. If terrorists had a bomb, they would probably not launch it on a missile. It is more likely that they would smuggle it into the United States, maybe in a cargo container. This type of nuclear weapon would likely be set off on the ground, if necessary at the price of a terrorist's own life. Missile defense could not prevent such an attack.

Also, politicians and military leaders have to consider that the current balance of power in the world is temporary. Right now, the United States has the strongest economy and military

force in the world. That probably won't last forever. In the future, the United States may face one or more powers of equal or greater strength. Will relations between the United States and these new superpowers be friendly or hostile? Only time will tell.

GLOSSARY

atom The basic particle that makes up everything in the universe. Atoms are made of three even smaller particles—electrons, protons, and neutrons.

ballistic missile A missile that is guided during its ascent and then falls freely during its descent to its target.

boost phase The first stage of a missile's flight, which takes the missile through Earth's atmosphere. The boost phase of a current intercontinental ballistic missile lasts between three to five minutes. It may be possible to reduce this period to around a minute.

Cold War The long conflict, short of outright war, between the United States and the Soviet Union during the second half of the twentieth century.

cruise missile A low-altitude, winged missile that flies under its own power through the atmosphere.

fission The splitting of an atomic nucleus, resulting in the release of large amounts of energy.

fusion The union of atomic nuclei to form heavier nuclei, resulting in the release of enormous quantities of energy.

geostationary orbit The movement of a satellite over Earth, circling the planet once a day in the direction of Earth's rotation.

global positioning system A system of satellites and receivers that allows the user to determine his or her exact location on Earth.

Intercontinental Ballistic Missile (ICBM) A long-range guided missile used for attack with nuclear weapons.

kinetic energy The energy of motion.

laser A device that creates a concentrated beam of electromagnetic radiation.

midcourse phase The longest period of a ballistic missile's flight, during which it travels outside the atmosphere.

neutron A particle without charge found in the center, or nucleus, of an atom.

nuclear weapon A weapon whose destructive power derives from an uncontrolled nuclear reaction.

payload Anything carried by a rocket or missile, such as a warhead, that is not is necessary for its operation.

postboost phase The period of a ballistic missile's flight between the time its engine drops off and the time it reaches the top of its trajectory.

proton A particle with a positive charge found in the center, or nucleus, of an atom.

radar A sensing device or system consisting of a radio transmitter and receiver, it generates radio waves that are reflected off the objects to be located.

Russian Federation An independent country in northeastern Europe and northern Asia made up of the core of the former Soviet Union.

Scud missile A Soviet missile used by the Iraqi military in the Iran-Iraq War (1980-1988) and the 1991 Gulf War ("Desert Storm").

Soviet Union The Union of Soviet Socialist Republics (USSR), a country established in 1922; America's principal opponent in the Cold War. The Soviet Union broke apart in 1991.

strategic defense Defense against long-range guided missiles armed with nuclear weapons.

Strategic Defense Initiative (SDI) A multibillion-dollar research project launched by the administration of U.S. president Ronald Reagan in the 1980s. Its aim was to develop military technologies that would provide a defense against ballistic missiles.

terminal phase The last phase of a ballistic missile's flight, during which it travels through the atmosphere toward its target.

warhead The weapon, usually nuclear, carried by a guided missile. A warhead could also carry a chemical or biological weapon.

X-ray laser A laser that emits a focused beam of extreme short-wave radiation.

FOR MORE INFORMATION

Arms Control Association
1150 Connecticut Avenue, NW
Suite 620
Washington, DC 20036
(202) 463-8270
Web site: http://www.armscontrol.org

Center for Defense Information
1779 Massachusetts Avenue NW
Washington, DC 20036-2109
(202) 332-0600
Web site: http://www.cdi.org

Federation of American Scientists
1717 K Street NW
Suite 209
Washington, DC 20036
(202) 546-3300
Web site: http://www.fas.org

Missile Defense Agency
Director, Communications
MDA/DC, The Pentagon
Washington, DC 20301-7100
(703) 697-8472
Web site: http://www.mda.mil

Raytheon Missile Defense
50 Apple Hill Drive, T3ME12
Tewksbury, MA 01876
(978) 858-5246
Web site: http://raytheonmissiledefense.com

U.S. Army Space and Missile Defense Command
P.O. Box 15280
Arlington, VA 22215-0280
(703) 607-2039
Web site: http://www.smdc.army.mil

Web Sites

Due to the changing nature of Internet links, the Rosen Publishing Group, Inc., has developed an online list of Web sites related to the subject of this book. This site is updated regularly. Please use this link to access the list:

http://www.rosenlinks.com/lfw/sdsf

FOR FURTHER READING

Allman, Toney. *J. Robert Oppenheimer.* San Diego, CA: Blackbirch Press, 2005.

Dartford, Mark. *Fighter Planes.* New York, NY: Lerner Publishing, 2003.

Dudley, William. *Missile Defense.* San Diego, CA: Greenhaven Press, 2002.

Gow, Catherine. *The Cuban Missile Crisis.* San Diego, CA: Lucent Books, 1997.

Lawton, Clive A. *Hiroshima: The Story of the First Atom Bomb.* Cambridge, MA: Candlewick, 2004.

Pitt, Matthew. *The Tomahawk Cruise Missile.* New York, NY: Children's Press, 2000.

Sherman, Josepha. *Cold War.* Minneapolis, MN: Lerner Publications, 2003.

Sherrow, Victoria. *The Making of the Atom Bomb.* San Diego, CA: Lucent Books, 2000.

Wolny, Philip. *Weapons Satellites.* New York, NY: Rosen Publishing Group, 2005.

BIBLIOGRAPHY

Broad, William J. *Teller's War: The Top-Secret Story Behind the Star Wars Deception.* New York, NY: Simon & Schuster, 1992.

Burns, Richard Dean, and Lester H. Brune. *The Quest for Missile Defenses, 1944–2003.* Claremont, CA: Regina Books, 2003.

Butler, Richard. *Fatal Choice: Nuclear Weapons and the Illusion of Missile Defense.* Boulder, CO: Westview Press, 2000.

Claremont Institute. "Chronology of Missile Defense." Retrieved June 13, 2005 (http://www.missilethreat.com/overview/chronology.html).

CNN Interactive. "Reagan's 'Star Wars' Speech." Retrieved June 13, 2005 (http://www.cnn.com/SPECIALS/ cold.war/episodes/22/documents/starwars.speech).

Handberg, Roger. *Ballistic Missile Defense and the Future of American Security.* Westport, CT: Praeger, 2002.

Hasegawa, Tsuyoshi. "Peaceful Coexistence and Detente." Retrieved June 13, 2005 (http://www.history.ucsb.edu/faculty/hasegawa/191/downloads/lecture11outline.pdf).

Lindsay, James M. *Defending America: The Case for Limited Missile Defense.* Washington, DC: Brookings Institution Press, 2000.

Missile Defense Agency. "Ballistic Missile Defense System:
A Historic Beginning." Retrieved August 15, 2005
(http://www.mda.mil/mdalink/pdf/bmdsbook.pdf).

Nordin, Yusof. *Space Warfare: High-Tech War of the Future
Generation.* Skudai, Johor Darul Ta'zim, Malaysia: Penerbit
Universiti Teknologi Malaysia, 1999.

Pahl, David. *Space Warfare and Strategic Defense.* New York, NY:
Exeter Books, 1987.

Walter, Katie. "The X-Ray Laser: From Underground to Tabletop."
Science and Technology Review, September 1998. Retrieved
August 15, 2005 (http://www.llnl.gov/str/Dunn.html).

INDEX

About the Author

Phillip Margulies is old enough to remember the air raid drills and fallout shelters of the early 1960s, when the big defense contractor a few miles from his home in Plainview, New York, was a presumed target of nuclear attack. He is the author of many books on history, science, and technology for young adults.

Photo Credits

Cover, pp. 7 and throughout, 22, 28–29, 36, 40 Ballistic Missile Defense System; cover (left corner) © Digital Vision/Getty Images; cover (top middle) © Photodisc Red/Getty Images; p. 9 © Corbis; p. 10 © Hulton-Deutsch Collection/Corbis; p. 12 © Jim Sugar/ Corbis; p. 17 © AP/Wide World Photos; p. 18 © Jeff Chiu/AP/Wide World Photos; p. 19 © Roger Ressmeyer/Corbis; p. 25 © Corbis; p. 30 © Rick Wilking/AP/Wide World Photos; pp. 32, 38 Department of Defense photo; pp. 35, 42, 45 Missile Defense Agency; pp. 48, 52 © Reuters/Corbis; p. 50 © B Calzada/ZUMA/Corbis.

Designer: Evelyn Horovicz; Editor: Brian Belval